D0242500

Penny on Safari

Cavan County Library
Withdrawn Stock

FABER-CASTELL
since 1761

Penny the Pencil has a proud heritage. She is made by the leading
pencil manufacturer in the world, Faber-Castell. The Faber-Castell
family have been making pencils for eight generations. It all started in
a small workshop in Germany in 1761 and now the company employs
5,500 people worldwide. The company is run by
Count Anton Wolfgang von Faber-Castell.

Faber-Castell is a company with great flair and vision. It is in the
Guinness Book of Records for creating the world's tallest pencil at
almost twenty metres high and has also made the most expensive
pencil ever. The Grip 2001 pencil brings together these elements of
design, quality and innovation. It has won many international awards.
With its unique soft grip zone and comfortable triangular shape it
has become a worldwide classic.

Penny on Safari

EILEEN O'HELY

Illustrated by Nicky Phelan

MERCIER PRESS
IRISH PUBLISHER - IRISH STORY

Main Characters

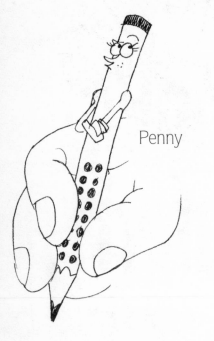

Penny

Zelda

Bu Hei

Black Texta

Milligan

Spike

Herby

Bob

Fionnuala

For Brendan

Contents

Chapter 1   **Art class**   **11**

Chapter 2   **Zoo excursion**   **24**

Chapter 3   **Safariddles**   **39**

Chapter 4   **Theft**   **55**

Chapter 5   **Black attack**   **69**

Chapter 6   **A touch of home**   **85**

Chapter 7   **The missing zebra**   **100**

Chapter 8   **Do feed the animals**   **114**

Chapter 9   **Petition**   **127**

Chapter 10   **The truth about Bert**   **144**

Chapter 11   **Showdown**   **159**

Chapter 12   **Karma restored**   **177**

Chapter 1

Art class

CAVAN COUNTY LIBRARY

'Quiet! Everybody in two rows. The bell's about to ring,' said a bottle of correction fluid as the pencils, rubbers, crayons and other writing implements in the pencil case jostled to get into position. The coloured pencils in particular were very excited, as the next lesson was Art.

The two lead pencils at the front of each row were also excited. Mack, the red mechanical pencil, was very good at drawing, so Ralph, the little red-haired boy whose pencil case it was, always used Mack to draw the outlines of his pictures. The other lead pencil, Penny, who had bubbles on her skirt, never made it out of the pencil case during Art class. She was so busy helping Ralph with his

Maths and Spelling and other lessons during the school week, that Art class was the one time she got to have a rest.

As the bell rang the tension inside the pencil case grew. Although the coloured pencils looked forward to Art class more than any other lesson, there was always the chance that Mrs Sword would let the children do an activity that didn't involve colouring in with pencils.

'I hope they're not doing painting again,' said Jade, Ralph's short green pencil. 'Especially since Ralph tends to get more paint on his school uniform than on the paper.'

'Charcoal's just as bad,' agreed Amber, Ralph's tall orange pencil. 'Grubby, black fingerprints all over everything.'

'And don't get me started on the time they did clay modelling ...' added Scarlett, Ralph's red pencil. She was the shortest of all the pencils because Ralph's favourite colour was red and he used Scarlett to colour in as often as possible.

'Just as well Ralph's mum has that stain remover that gets dirty marks out of anything,' added Smudge, Ralph's little lop-sided rubber. As a rubber, he was very impressed with anything that could clean as well or better than he could.

'Shhh!' whispered the bottle of correction fluid. 'Ralph's opening the zip!'

Mack shuffled forward as tooth by tooth the zip opened and Ralph's hand plunged into the pencil case. Ralph's fingers curled around Mack and he was lifted out into the classroom.

As Mack's toe disappeared through the zip, Penny reached up and gave it a little tickle. Mack, who was very ticklish, let out a yelp.

'Penny …' said the bottle of correction fluid sternly.

'Oh, relax, Gloop,' said Penny. 'Humans can't hear us when we talk. Or laugh.'

'But dey can ee us when we moobe!' said Gloop, without moving his lips.

'Only if they're looking,' said Penny, watching Ralph carefully and doing a little dance to tease Gloop. She stopped boogieing immediately as Ralph's hand entered the pencil case again.

'Yippee!' said Hazel, Ralph's brown pencil, as she disappeared through the zip.

'Woohoo!' said Jade a moment later, as Ralph's hand lifted her out of the pencil case.

'Brown and green,' said Smudge. 'What do you think Ralph's drawing?'

'A peppermint ice-cream cone,' suggested Penny.

'I reckon it's the Finbarr Hurlers football team!' said Smudge, who was a big fan of the team in the green-and-brown-striped jerseys.

'What do you think, Gloop?' asked Penny.

'Given what the children were learning in class earlier in the week, I'd say he's drawing a –'

But before Gloop could finish, Ralph's hand entered the pencil case again. Instead of rummaging through the coloured pencils, it was

making a bee-line for Smudge, Gloop and Penny.

'Oh no,' said Smudge. 'I hope Ralph hasn't coloured in outside the lines again. I'm not very good at rubbing out coloured pencil,' he said, looking at his left side, which was not only lop-sided but every colour of the rainbow.

Luckily for Smudge, Ralph's fingers went past the little rubber, past Gloop and curled around Penny instead.

'Don't tell me Art class is over and it's time for Spelling already,' said Penny as Ralph lifted her out of the pencil case.

The last thing she heard was Gloop saying: 'Just as I thought. With brown, green and grey, Ralph must be drawing a ...'

'*Grey* in the picture?' thought Penny. She prided herself on being a serious lessons pencil, rather than just one of the coloured pencils.

As Ralph started colouring with her, Penny looked at the picture and started to enjoy herself. Ralph had drawn a jungle scene, full of trees with dark green leaves and thick brown trunks. He was

using Penny to colour in a very odd-shaped animal in the centre of the picture. It was very big, with legs wider than the tree trunks and huge, floppy ears. Most unusual of all was that the animal seemed to have two tails: a short, skinny one at what Penny thought was its back, and a long, wide one at its front, between two tusks.

It wasn't until Ralph was half-way through colouring in the animal that Penny worked out what it was. An elephant!

When Ralph had finished colouring in the elephant, he laid Penny down on the desk and grabbed more coloured pencils from his pencil case. By the end of Art class there was a jungle full of animals: monkeys, tigers and, most surprising of all, a peacock!

Ralph took his picture up to Mrs Sword for marking. The queue of children to the teacher's desk was very long. As usual, Ralph's best friend Sarah was first in line.

'That's an excellent picture, Sarah,' said Mrs Sword, writing a big A+ on the top corner of Sarah's picture of African animals gathered around a watering hole. Penny thought the teacher's writing ruined the picture, but Sarah looked quite pleased about it.

The boy in line behind Ralph sniggered. Ralph
turned around. It was Bert, the class bully.

'Leave Sarah alone,' Ralph said.

'Oh, I'm not laughing at *her*,' said Bert nastily,
eyeing Ralph's drawing, 'I'm laughing at *you*!'

19

'Why?' said Ralph, turning his drawing over.

'Because there aren't any peacocks in Africa,' said Bert.

'This isn't a picture of Africa, it's a picture of an Indian jungle,' said Ralph.

'Then why does your elephant have big ears?' sneered Bert.

'Elephants have big ears!' said Ralph hotly.

'Not all elephants,' said Bert. 'African elephants have big ears and Indian elephants have small ears.'

'You're very well informed about elephants, Bert,'

20

said Sarah, who had made her way back from Mrs Sword's desk. 'Don't tell me you've been to the Proboscidea exhibition at the museum.'

'The what?' asked Ralph.

'Oh, yeah. Like I'd go to the museum if I didn't have to,' said Bert, turning a slight tinge of red. 'I might catch nerd germs from bumping into you there,' he added, shoving Sarah deliberately.

Ralph stepped between them.

'If you're not a museum nerd,' said Ralph, ignoring the look Sarah shot him, 'how do you know so much about elephants?'

Bert paused for a minute, then narrowed his eyes.

'From playing *Safari Shoot-Up* on X-Station. The African elephants are easier targets. Bigger ears.'

Bert reached out to grab Ralph's ear.

'Ow!' wailed Bert, as someone pinched his ear instead.

'Bert O'Leary!' said Mrs Sword, marching Bert by the ear to the front of the classroom. 'Go straight to the principal's office. I'll let him be the judge of whether your behaviour stops you from

going on our excursion next week.'

'What excursion?' asked Lucy Williams, the girl who sat in front of Ralph and Sarah.

'I'll give you a hint,' said Mrs Sword. 'The theme of today's Art class is exotic animals.'

'The Far East,' said Malcolm, naming the most exotic place he could think of, despite

the fact that the 'exotic' animal he had drawn was a squirrel.

'Not quite that far,' said Mrs Sword.

'The Middle East,' said Seán, who had drawn a picture of a camel.

'Getting closer,' said Mrs Sword. 'But we don't have to catch a plane to get there.'

Sarah put her hand up. 'I know. The zoo!'

'That's right,' said Mrs Sword, handing out permission slips for the children to take home.

Chapter 2

Zoo excursion

On the morning of the excursion, Classroom 3B sounded more like a beehive than a classroom. The children were absolutely buzzing with excitement about their trip to the zoo.

'I can't wait to see Bu Hei, the baby albino panda,' said Ciara, the girl who sat next to Lucy Williams.

'Is that a panda from Albania?' asked Seán.

'No, it's a panda that's white all over,' laughed Ciara.

'Wouldn't that be a polar bear?'

'They're different species,' snapped Sarah, who was excited at having a day off classes, but was sorry they were missing double Geometry.

Inside Ralph's pencil case the writing
implements had mixed feelings about the excursion
too.

'I hate excursions,' said Penny.

'Really?' said Mack in surprise. 'I like 'em. With
our owners out of the classroom for the whole day
we get to go pencil case hopping and catch up with
all the other children's pencils. I haven't seen Fleur
since the Pencilympics.'

'As long as none of Bert's pencils think they can hop into our pencil case,' said Smudge.

'Oh, it's not that,' said Penny. 'I have to admit I'm quite looking forward to having a chat with Polly myself. It's just that the spelling test was supposed to be today. Now it won't be until after the weekend ...'

'There's more to life than spelling tests,' said Gloop. 'The children will learn far more by going to the zoo and seeing the animals in action than they would just reading about them in a book and learning how to spell their names.'

Penny, Mack and Smudge all looked at Gloop in surprise. It was

26

most unlike him to defend anything that wasn't classroom-based learning.

'Okay,' said Penny, once she had gotten over her shock. 'If excursions are so important, why don't we ever get to go –'

But before Penny could finish, Mack, Smudge, Gloop and all the coloured pencils crowded in on top of her.

'Whoooooooa!' said all the writing implements as, pencil case and all, they were lifted into the air.

'What's happening?' asked Rose, Ralph's pink-coloured pencil.

'It would seem that Penny's wish has been granted,' said Gloop, 'and we're on our way to the zoo!'

Penny couldn't have been happier and led the entire pencil case in a chorus of 'We're Going to the Zoo' and then 'The Wheels on the Bus' all the way to the zoo.

When Ralph lifted the pencil case out of his backpack, all the pencils crowded around the zip to be the first to look at the animals.

'Everybody, please! Take your places,' said Gloop, having to shout over the excited voices. 'We may not be in the classroom, but we still have to follow the Rules.'

At the mention of the Rules, the writing implements shuffled quietly into two neat rows and stood very still. As the zip began to open, a beam of sunlight entered the pencil case, dazzling both Mack and Penny who were closest to the zip. Penny was squinting so hard that she didn't realise Ralph's hand had entered the pencil case until she felt a warm thumb and index finger close around her waist and lift her out into the fresh air.

But the air was hardly fresh.

'What's that bad smell?' asked Ralph.

Penny held a hand up to shield her eyes and had

a look around. She was in an outdoor auditorium with a view over the elephant enclosure. Mrs Sword was making her way between the children, passing out activity sheets.

'I think it's what just came out of that elephant's bottom,' said Sarah, screwing up her nose.

'I thought it was you,' said Bert.

'Bert!' said Mrs Sword sharply, rapping him over the head with the remaining activity sheets. 'You're lucky to be on this excursion as it is. One more word like that out of you and you'll find yourself mucking out the elephant pen for the rest of the day.'

Before Bert could protest, the children at the front of the auditorium started clapping. A man in khaki-coloured shorts and a matching short-sleeved shirt had burst onto the stage.

'Good morning Threebee!' he boomed. 'My name's Bob and I'm the Head Keeper here at Kilknock Zoo. Hands up who's been to the zoo before?'

Everyone put their hand up (apart from Lucy Williams whose family days out were always excursions to the chocolate factory).

'That's what I like to see,' said Bob. 'This trip to the zoo will be different to all the others, because today we'll be going on safari!'

'Ooh,' said the class.

'What sort of animals do you think we'll see on our zoo safari?' Bob asked.

'Elephants,' said Ralph.

'Zultan the Sumatran tiger,' said Seán.

'Giraffes,' said Malcolm.

'Australian marsupials,' said Sarah.

'Marsupial,' said Bob. 'That's a big word for a little girl. Would you like to tell your classmates what a marsupial is?'

'It's an animal that has a pouch for its young, like a kangaroo,' said Sarah proudly.

'Very good,' said Bob, beaming at Sarah. 'What other animals could we expect to see?'

'The albino panda,' said Ciara.

'That's right!' said Bob, even more enthusiastically.

'Kilknock Zoo has a brand new baby albino panda, Bu Hei, one of only two in the world!'

'Ooh!' said the class again.

'Now,' continued Bob, 'I won't be leading you around the zoo on safari. You'll be leading yourselves, guided by safariddles.'

'What's a safariddle?' asked Ralph.

'It's a riddle that tells you which animal to see next,' explained Bob. 'If you look at the sheets your teacher handed out to you, you'll see there's a map of the zoo. But instead of having the names of the animals marked on the individual enclosures, it's divided into sections like Oriental Ursines and Flightless Feathered Friends. Your project today is to write the names of the safari animals in their correct enclosures. The safariddles will guide you from one animal to the next.'

'But there's only one riddle on the page,' said Seán.

'That's right,' said Bob. 'If you solve the riddle correctly, when you get to that animal's enclosure you'll find another safariddle to lead you to the next animal.'

'Boooo-ring,' muttered Bert.

'Is that a question in the back there?' asked Bob, looking directly at Bert.

'Why bother solving riddles?' said Bert. 'Why can't we just walk around the zoo and fill in the map by looking at the animals?'

'You could do that,' said Bob. 'But not all the animals are that easy to see. We've tried to recreate the animals' natural habitats in their enclosures, so there are lots of rocks and trees and places for the animals to hide. Also, some are very good at camouflage, while others are nocturnal and don't like to venture out much during the day.'

Bert made a little yapping gesture with his hand during Bob's explanation.

'If it sounds too easy,' said Bob, looking Bert in the eye, 'maybe you'd like to tell the class the difference between an okapi and an impala.'

'Both are African animals, but okapis live in the rainforest, have dark brown bodies and striped legs,' began Bert, 'while impalas live on grasslands, are pale brown and have horns.'

The whole class, including Mrs Sword and Bob, gaped at Bert.

'Or … something like that,' muttered Bert, trying not to appear too smart.

'What's this mystery phrase down at the bottom?' asked Sarah, who always read on ahead, even on excursions, and quite disliked the fact that Bert knew more about African animals than she did.

'I was just coming to that,' said Bob. 'You need to write the first letter of each animal on our zoo safari in the boxes at the bottom of the page to spell a mystery phrase.'

'Ahh!' said the class (apart from Bert), liking the idea of solving the mystery phrase as much as the safariddles.

'I can see you're all dying to get on with things,' said Bob, clapping his hands together, 'so keep to the paths, don't feed the animals and enjoy your day at the zoo!'

Rather than leaping up to run to the first animal on the safari, the children stayed seated, trying to work out the riddle. Penny could just read the wording over Ralph's wrist:

Weighing well over a tonne

I live in the African sun

I like to wallow in the mud

My ugly face will cool your blood.

Penny had barely finished reading the safariddle

when she felt a strong jolt.

'Come on!' shouted Sarah, leaping up with her

map and safariddle sheet in one hand and Ralph's

jacket collar in the other. 'I've worked it out. Let's get there before the others do.'

And with that, Ralph, Sarah and their pencils began their safari.

Chapter 3

Safariddles

'Where are we going?' puffed Ralph, finding it hard to keep up with Sarah.

'Shhh!' shushed Sarah. 'We're not far away enough yet. Someone might hear.'

Ralph bent over to catch his breath, his head down between his legs.

'Sarah,' he said, upside-down. 'I can see all the way back to the auditorium, and no one's coming.'

'Oh,' said Sarah, double-checking. 'In that case we're heading to African Megafauna.'

'How did you get a gigantic African baby deer from that clue?' asked Ralph. 'Besides, I thought baby deer were cute.'

'Not megafaun, megafaun-A!' said Sarah,

pausing in front of an enclosure. 'And here we are.'

Ralph looked behind Sarah and saw a herd of hippopotami wallowing in the mud.

'Of course!' he said. 'Hippos!'

Ralph used Penny to write a capital H in the first box of the mystery phrase.

'And here's the next safariddle,' said Sarah, pointing to a sheet of paper tacked up on the edge of the hippo information board:

When I want a tasty treat
I find a nest of ants to eat
My nose is long, my tongue is sticky
Spelling my name is very tricky

'Tricky to spell?' mused Sarah, who, like Penny, was very good at spelling.

'Hmmm,' said Ralph, who was a bad speller, 'some sort of anteater?'

'Echidnas eat ants!' said Sarah. 'How do you spell echidna, Ralph?'

'Um …' said Ralph. 'E-K-'

Penny rolled her eyes.

'That's definitely it!' said Sarah, grabbing Ralph by the hand and dragging him towards Australian Marsupials.

But surprisingly, when they got to the echidna enclosure there was no safariddle.

'That's strange,' said Sarah. 'I was sure it was an echidna. They eat ants. It says so right here,' she continued, pointing to the information board. 'Diet: Ants.'

'I hate to say it,' said Ralph, trying very hard to keep a straight face, 'but this could be one of those rare occasions when you're wrong.'

Sarah glared at Ralph.

'Okay then, Mr Smarty Pants,' huffed Sarah, 'what other ant-eating animal could it be?'

'Um … it could be a … a … uh …' began Ralph.

'All right, all right,' said Sarah, rolling her eyes and looking at her zoo map grumpily. 'No need to rub it in.'

'No need to rub what in?' said Ralph.

'A-A-R-D-V-A-R-K. Aardvark,' said Sarah, refusing to look at him.

Ralph stared at her.

'You thought I was spelling aardvark?' he asked.

'Weren't you?' said Sarah, looking up sharply.

'Of course I was,' said Ralph, blushing and pretending to study his map.

'African Insectivores this way,' said Sarah, dashing off.

Just as they arrived at African Insectivores, Malcolm and Seán rushed out, then proceeded to run in different directions.

'Polar Birds this way,' yelled Seán.

'That's the way to Polar *Bears*, not Polar *Birds*,' said Malcolm. 'We want Antarctic Animals.'

Seán studied his map for a second, then turned and ran after Malcolm.

Ralph and Sarah went to find the aardvark. It

was very easy, as there was a large group of their classmates gathered in front of it.

'Tsk,' tsked Sarah when she saw how many of their classmates had overtaken them because of her mistake.

'Let's go, Ciara!' said Lucy, turning around and almost crashing into Sarah. 'Sorry, Sarah. I didn't see you … hang on, why are you going that way?'

'We, em, took a detour,' said Sarah, trying to hide her flushing cheeks.

'Did you say detour, or *mistake*?' sneered Bert, sidling up behind Sarah.

'Yes, we went to visit your relatives in the monkey house,' said Ralph. 'Come on, Sarah,' he added, guiding Sarah away from Bert and the aardvark.

'Ralph, the aardvark's that way,' said Sarah.

'But we need to go this way,' said Ralph.

'But the safariddle's that way,' protested Sarah.

'I know. I've read it,' said Ralph.

'But shouldn't I read it too?' said Sarah. 'I mean, it's not like we haven't made any mistakes so far today ...' she mumbled.

'All right,' said Ralph impatiently. 'I'll tell it to you on the way to the penguins:

My first are something with which you write

My last start a drink dark as night

The way I walk is quite absurd

I am a polar swimming bird.'

'Polar swimming bird is obviously a penguin,' said
Sarah. 'But what about the first three lines? I mean,
we don't want to be caught out like last time …'

Ralph took a deep breath.

'Well, you write with a pen,' he began, 'and
Guinness is a drink that's dark as night …'

'… and the first four letters of Guinness are the
last four letters of penguin!' said Sarah excitedly.
'Some of the others are already there. What are you
waiting for?'

She dashed off, with Ralph shaking his head
behind her.

When they reached the penguin enclosure, the
children already gathered there didn't seem the least

interested in solving the next safariddle. They were
too busy watching the penguins, who were putting
on an excellent show. A steady stream of penguins
was waddling up the side of an ice hillock where a
group was already gathered. Each time one of the
climbing penguins got to the top, he'd push and
shove to join the group. All the other penguins
would waddle around until one of them lost their
footing and plummeted belly-first over the edge.
That penguin would continue surfing down the

hillock and across the ice before landing in the water with a big splash. Then he'd swim to the edge, clamber out, shake off his feathers and join the queue waddling to the top of the hillock again.

'I'd love to be a penguin,' said Ciara. 'Nothing to do but swim and slide around all day.'

'But you'd have to eat raw fish,' said Lucy.

'That's okay. I like sushi,' said Ciara.

'Speaking of having nothing to do,' Sarah whispered to Ralph, 'we'd better work out the next safariddle.'

Ralph and Sarah wrote a 'P' in the third box of their mystery phrase, then inched their way through the crowd of children to read the safariddle:

I'm an oriental bear
Half of me black, half of me fair
I like munching on bamboo
It is my favourite thing to do

'Oriental Ursines, here we come!' said Sarah.

They hurried through Jungle Cats and Exotic Birds, and were the first to arrive at the panda enclosure.

'Here's the riddle,' said Ralph, writing a 'P' with Penny in the fourth box of his mystery phrase. '*I'm a type of shaggy cow —*'

'Who cares?' said Sarah, her face pressed up against the glass, gazing at the pandas.

'Eh?' said Ralph.

'We're the first ones here,' said Sarah, not taking her eyes from the pandas. 'We can relax and watch the pandas for a while. Now where's the albino one got to?'

'Bob said it's brand new, so it'll be the smallest one,' said Ralph, trying to spot a little white panda among the bamboo.

Ralph and Sarah were so busy looking for the baby panda that they didn't hear the whir of a zoo

maintenance vehicle drive up behind them.

'Crikey! What are you two doing here already?'

Ralph and Sarah span around to see Bob sitting in the driver's seat.

'You've solved four safariddles already?' continued Bob. 'Don't tell me they're too easy!'

'Definitely not,' said Ralph. 'Sarah's the

smartest girl in school and even she got one wro
– ow!'

Ralph rubbed his shin where Sarah had kicked
it.

'Smartest girl in school, eh?' said Bob. 'Which
one did you get wrong?'

'It was an ambiguous clue,' said Sarah
defensively. 'I thought the hard-to-spell anteater
was an echidna –'

'Blimey! It could have been too!' said Bob. 'Well,
there's no point changing it now,' he added glumly.

'It's obviously too late for our class,' said Sarah.
'But when another school comes to visit …'

'No other schools are coming to visit,' said Bob
sadly.

'Why not?' asked Ralph.

'Because the zoo's closing.'

'Closing?!' said Ralph and Sarah together. 'Why?'

'It costs a lot to run a zoo,' explained Bob.

'There's all the animal
food and keepers' wages and
repairs to the enclosures ... So
the Mayor's going to sell the zoo.'

'Who to?' asked Sarah.

'Penz Inc.,' said Bob. 'They're going to tear down
the zoo and build a texta factory.'

Penny poked her head up at the mention of the
word 'texta'.

'A texta factory?' said Ralph. 'But the animals
can't live in a texta factory. What's going to happen
to them?'

'We're trying to get them adopted by other zoos,' said Bob. 'But we haven't had a lot of success so far.'

'When's the zoo closing?' asked Sarah.

'Unless we can come up with a bright idea, the end of next week,' said Bob.

'Sarah's clever. She'll think of something,' said Ralph hopefully.

'Even so, it would have to be an absolutely brilliant plan. They've already started delivering texta-making supplies,' said Bob, nodding to a stack of large, black drums piled up just inside the gate.

'*Alpha-one, alpha-one, you're needed urgently at the elephant enclosure,*' hissed a voice from the dashboard.

'Gotta go, elephant emergency!' said Bob.

And with a whir, he was off.

Ralph and Sarah stood staring at the panda exhibit, trying to come up with a brilliant plan. They barely noticed a voice next to them reading the next safariddle aloud:

I'm a type of shaggy cow

My horns are sharp – be careful – ow!

Not an ideal household pet

I'm from the highlands of Tibet.

'Don't tell me you two haven't worked it out yet.'

Ralph and Sarah turned to see Bert smirking at them.

'Well, can't stand around *yakking* with you losers all day,' said Bert over his shoulder as he headed off in the direction of Highland Ruminants.

From Ralph's back pocket, Penny watched Bert leave with a very nervous feeling in her tummy. Wherever Bert went, Black Texta wasn't far behind. And if Black Texta had heard Bob talking about the zoo being turned into a texta factory, Penny was sure he'd do everything in his power to make sure it happened.

Chapter 4

Theft

Penny had to wait until lunchtime to share the dreadful news with her friends in the pencil case. Despite Bert's clue, it had taken Ralph and Sarah a long time to work out that the shaggy Tibetan cow was a yak.

'Hippo, Aardvark, Penguin, Panda and Yak,' said Sarah. 'That makes the first word of the mystery phrase: HAPPY. Shall we stop for lunch?'

'Yeah!' said Ralph, tossing Penny into the pencil case and unwrapping his sandwiches.

'What's wrong, Penny?' asked Mack, as Ralph's hand deposited a very jittery Penny through the zip.

'He's back ... zoo closing ... texta factory ...' stuttered Penny.

'Calm down,' said Gloop. 'Now take a deep breath and tell us one thing at a time.'

'He's back. Black Texta is back,' said Penny.

All the writing implements let out a horrified gasp, apart from Gloop who was frowning with his mouth tightly shut.

'He's going to close the zoo and build an enormous texta factory in its place!' finished Penny.

Half of the coloured pencils fainted, and Mack and Smudge started to shake.

'Hold on, hold on,' said Gloop, putting his hand up for silence. 'Penny, what proof do you have that

Black Texta's back? And what makes you think he's going to turn the zoo into a texta factory?'

'I heard Bob the Head Keeper talking to Ralph and Sarah about it,' began Penny.

'Did this Head Keeper specifically mention Black Texta?' interrupted Gloop.

'No,' said Penny. 'But Bert was eavesdropping and Black Texta –'

'Penny,' interrupted Gloop again, noticing more and more coloured pencils fainting at every mention of Black Texta,  'when was the last time you saw Black Texta?'

'At Space Camp,' answered Penny.

'And what did he look like?' continued Gloop.

'He was bigger and meaner and musclier –'

'No,' said Gloop. 'What did he look like the *very last* time you saw him?'

'You mean in the rocket exhaust? When he was just a bubbling, black mass of charred plastic?' asked Penny.

'Precisely!' said Gloop, turning away from Penny to reassure the coloured pencils. 'I admit that Black Texta has had some close calls in the past and has managed to come back from some decidedly sticky endings, but we all saw him disintegrate in the rocket fumes with our own eyes. There's no way he could have survived that.'

All the coloured pencils breathed a huge sigh of relief, and some of them even whispered to each other and laughed in Penny's direction. Only Mack and Smudge gave Penny sympathetic looks to show they agreed with her.

With a satisfied nod, Gloop turned away from the crowd.

'You three, come with me,' he said, leading Penny, Mack and Smudge to a quiet corner of the pencil case. 'What else did this Head Keeper have to say about the texta factory?'

'Why are you so interested?' Penny asked angrily. 'It's not like you believe Black Texta's back.'

'Oh, yes I do,' said Gloop quietly.

'Huh?' said Penny.

'His plastic may have melted, but Black Texta's evil to the core,' continued Gloop. 'If any of his ink cartridge survived, then he may very well still be out there.'

Smudge let out a frightened little squeak.

'Then what was that big speech back there all about?' asked Mack.

'I said what I said to keep the coloured pencils calm,' said Gloop. 'You know what an excitable bunch they are. Why, half of them fainted at the mere mention of the name Black Texta. Can you imagine the chaos in here if they thought he was really back?'

'Forget the pencil case. Imagine the chaos *everywhere* if Black Texta has his own personal army of textas being manufactured just down the road from Ralph and Sarah's school!' squeaked Smudge.

'One step at a time,' said Gloop. 'Now, Penny, did Bob say anything else that Bert may have overheard?'

'I'm not sure how long Bert was there,' said Penny. 'He might have also heard Bob say that some texta supplies have already been delivered.'

'Where exactly were they delivered?' asked Gloop.

'Near the panda enclosure,' said Penny.

'Then that's where we should start,' said Gloop.

'But how are we going to get there?' asked Penny. 'Ralph and Sarah have already been to the panda –'

'I know!' said Mack.

But Penny didn't hear what he had to say as a thumb and forefinger closed around her and she was pulled out of the dark pencil case into the bright sunlight. Lunchtime was obviously over. Penny blinked and found herself in front of a dry, grassy enclosure where a black and white horse was trotting around.

'See?' said Sarah proudly, writing a Z in the next box of her mystery phrase. 'I told you

I am a kind of stripey horse
I come from Africa of course
My name begins with a letter rare
And ends with women's underwear

meant zebra!'

'Well that was pretty obvious from the first line. You don't have to keep going on about women's underwear and stuff,' mumbled Ralph.

'Here's the next one,' said Sarah, enjoying Ralph's embarrassment. 'Go ahead and read it.'

Grudgingly Ralph read the safariddle to himself before reading it aloud, just in case it had something even worse in it than a bra:

I'm the kind that likes to swing
Bananas are my favourite thing
Rainforests are my habitat
My fur is orange and that's that.

'That's got to be an orangutan,' said Sarah. 'Sumatran Simeons here we come!'

Ralph and Sarah raced each other to the orangutan enclosure. The next safariddle was taped to the information board. Ralph wrote an 'O' in the seventh box of his mystery phrase which now read 'HAPPY ZO_ _ _ _ _ _ _' and started reading through the new safariddle, which turned out to be really easy.

'I know what it i-is!' Ralph told Sarah in a singsong voice.

'Shh!' shushed Sarah.

'All right,' said Ralph. 'But I thought you were the one in the hurry to solve the mystery phrase –'

'Who cares about the mystery phrase?' said Sarah, not taking her eyes off the information board.

'*I* don't,' said Bert, waltzing past and flapping his activity sheet in Sarah's face. 'I've already finished. Enjoy the rest of your *zoo safari*!'

But Sarah paid Bert no attention and turned to Ralph.

'These beautiful animals are critically endangered,' she said with tears in her eyes. 'There's only a few thousand of them left in the wild.'

Ralph looked at the orangutans. Most of them were playing, but one was eyeing him quite curiously.

'Why are they endangered? They look healthy enough to me,' said Ralph.

'Not these ones,' tutted Sarah. 'The ones in the wild. Their habitat's being destroyed, meaning they don't have enough food or shelter … and some of them are hunted for illegal trade, or worse!'

The curious orangutan came up close to Ralph and Sarah.

'Look,' said Sarah. 'He just wants to be our friend.'

Suddenly, the orangutan reached through the bars towards Ralph and snatched Penny out of his hand.

'Hey! That's my pencil! Give it back!' yelled Ralph as the orangutan ran with Penny to the back of the enclosure.

'Hey! I'm Ralph's pencil! Give me back!' yelled Penny at the same time.

The orangutan looked Penny in the eye and said, 'No.'

Penny blinked, stunned.

'You … you … you can talk!' she stammered.

'Of course,' said the orangutan.

'And … and … you can hear me when I talk?' babbled Penny.

'Naturally,' said the orangutan.

'But … but … how?'

'All animals can talk,' explained the orangutan, with a highly amused expression on his face.

'Good to know,' said Penny. 'Now give me back to Ralph.'

'I can't do that,' said the orangutan.

'Sure you can,' said Penny. 'You just walk over to the bars and put me back in Ralph's hand with an apology. Hang on, better leave out the apology. It might freak him out …'

'No,' said the orangutan.

'Why not?' asked Penny.

A second orangutan with a grey beard and sad eyes walked up to Penny and said, 'Because we need your help.'

Chapter 5

Black attack

'Oh, yeah?' said Penny. 'Well Ralph needs my help to solve the safarid – hang on, you need *my* help?'

'Yes,' said Greybeard. 'We're in danger.'

'I know you're endangered, I read the sign,' said Penny. 'And I know the fact that I'm a wooden pencil means I'm somehow partly responsible for deforestation –'

'I'm not just talking about orangutans,' interrupted Greybeard.

'I know. There was a bit on the sign about deforestation affecting elephants and tigers –'

'I'm not talking about deforestation, serious problem though it is,' said Greybeard. 'I'm talking about all the animals in Kilknock Zoo.'

69

'You're *all* going extinct?' gasped Penny.

'We will if the texta factory gets built,' said Rob, the orangutan who'd stolen Penny in the first place.

'Oh,' said Penny.

'Your reputation as a texta tamer precedes you,' said Greybeard.

'My *reputation*?' said Penny. 'But how …?'

'Word gets around,' said Greybeard.

'Especially when a celebrity like yourself makes it into *Monkey See, Monkey Do*,' said Rob.

'What's *Monkey See, Monkey Do*?' asked Penny.

'The zoo's number one selling entertainment magazine,' explained Rob. 'If you stick a load of monkeys and typewriters in the same room, they come out with things a

lot more interesting than the complete works of Shakespeare.'

'If you've quite finished,' said Greybeard in an almost Gloop-like manner, 'we do have more pressing matters than monkey press.'

Penny and Rob grew quiet, and the other orangutans gathered around to listen.

'Now, Penny,' said Greybeard. 'I'm not sure if you're aware of the possibility of the zoo being turned into a texta factory …'

'I'd say it's more than a possibility,' said Penny. 'They've already started delivering the supplies.'

'They've what?'

'When?'

'How do you know this?' said all of the orangutans at once.

'I overheard the Head Keeper talking to my owner and I saw the supply tanks by the panda enclosure with my very own eyes,' said Penny.

'Then it's even more serious than I thought,' said Greybeard.

'Why didn't the pandas tell us?' asked Rob.

'Do you think they pay attention to anything other than bamboo?' sniffed Henna, the first female orangutan Penny had heard speak.

'Enough!' said Greybeard, holding up a hand for order. 'Since you are so well-informed,' he said to Penny, 'I take it you already have a plan of action?'

'Not exactly,' admitted Penny. 'But the tanks near the panda enclosure could be a good place to start.'

'No problem,' said Greybeard. 'Fearful Fionnuala'll be heading to the panda enclosure shortly.'

'Who's Fearful Fionnuala?' asked Penny, looking around at the assembled orangutans.

'She's not one of us,' said Rob. 'She's a keeper.'

'Why is she called Fearful Fionnuala?' asked Penny.

All the orangutans looked at each other and smirked, even Greybeard, who, until then, Penny had thought too dignified to smirk.

'She's called Fearful Fionnuala because she's scared of all the animals,' explained Greybeard.

'Even Herby!' said Rob, and all the orangutans burst out laughing.

'Shh!' said Greybeard, as a set of keys jingled in the lock.

The door opened very slowly and a boot gingerly poked into the enclosure. It was followed by the leg and skinny body of a lady only slightly taller than Sarah, and a lot less brave.

'Nice monkeys … here's your food …' said Fearful Fionnuala.

'We're not monkeys, we're orangutans!' huffed Henna.

'Shh! You're frightening her! I need to ask her if she'll take Penny to the panda enclosure for us,' said Rob, lumbering up towards Fearful Fionnuala with Penny in his outstretched arms.

But being human, Fearful Fionnuala couldn't understand a word the animals were saying. All she heard and saw was a buffoonery of orangutans, with one of them charging towards her. She turned and ran screaming to the door.

Rob reached out and only just managed to ram Penny into Fearful Fionnuala's back pocket as she disappeared out of the enclosure.

'No! Not the back pocket!' cried Penny.

But it was too late. The door was locked and Penny was sandwiched in between the two layers of fabric that made up Fearful Fionnuala's back pocket.

As Penny crawled back up the pocket and poked her head out, she felt a familiar vibration and an accompanying bad smell.

'Oh no,' sighed Penny, grabbing her nose with one hand and fanning the air with the other. 'Maybe they should call her Flatulent Fionnuala instead!'

Penny heard a door open and Fearful Fionnuala tiptoed into another enclosure. There was a strange, chewing sort of noise accompanied by a rumbling *amboobamboobamboob*.

'Nice bearies,' said Fearful Fionnuala as she crept around the enclosure doing her zoo keeper duties (and also doing lots of bottom vibrations with accompanying foul smells).

Finally Fearful
Fionnuala turned
around and Penny
could see clumps
of bamboo and the
occasional black paw.

'The panda
enclosure!' breathed
Penny.

And breathe she could, because Fearful
Fionnuala's bottom had finally stopped vibrating
and the air was clear. It was only then that Penny
noticed the smell. A smell that made her feel even
sicker than if she'd been in the back pocket of
someone who'd just eaten curried baked beans. It
was a strong smell, a black, inky smell that could
mean only one thing.

'I'm too late. He's been here already,' sighed
Penny.

She wriggled her way up to the very top of
Fearful Fionnuala's pocket and jumped out without
the keeper noticing. Penny landed in a clump
of bamboo and shuffled from clump to clump,
following the inky smell.

The closer Penny got to the far corner, the
stronger the inky smell became.

'That's either Black Texta, or …'

Penny let out a gasp. A tiny panda was rolling

about, munching on bamboo. It looked just like a regular panda, white all over with black fur around its eyes and paws. But as Penny drew closer she noticed the panda's eyes were blue instead of dark brown.

'Bu Hei?' said Penny.

The little panda looked up.

'Not any more, bamboo bamboo,' it said, barely pausing from its bamboo eating.

'What do you mean?' asked Penny.

'In my country "bu hei" means no black, bamboo bamboo,' said Bu Hei. 'But now I'm black in all the right places, bamboo bamboo.'

'Don't worry, Bu Hei. I'll get the guy who did this to you,' said Penny.

'Please pass him my thanks, bamboo bamboo,' said Bu Hei.

'Your *thanks*?' said Penny.

'Yes, bamboo bamboo. Now I look like a real panda, bamboo bamboo.'

Penny was about to argue, when a long-clawed paw picked her up. Two large, dark brown eyes looked at her curiously.

'You're a strange-looking piece of bamboo, bamboo bamboo,' said the largest panda Penny had ever seen, holding Penny dangerously close to her mouth.

'I'm not bamboo,' said Penny. 'I'm a pencil.'

The panda looked at her blankly.

'I'm a pencil, *bamboo bamboo*,' said Penny.

'If you're not bamboo and you're certainly not a panda, what are you doing in our enclosure, bamboo bamboo?' asked the large panda.

'Trying to stop the fiend who did this,' said Penny, pointing to Bu Hei. 'Bamboo bamboo,' she added.

'Why, bamboo bamboo?' asked the large panda.

'Bu Hei looks like a proper panda now, bamboo bamboo. Now there won't be so many people coming and pointing, bamboo bamboo. We will have to think of a new name for her though, bamboo bamboo.'

'Unless we catch this guy then there won't be any people coming at all because the zoo will close!' said Penny.

The pandas looked at her blankly.

'Bamboo bamboo,' added Penny.

The pandas just shrugged and went back to their bamboo eating.

'Bu Hei, bamboo bamboo,' said Penny desperately. 'What did the guy who did this to you look like, bamboo bamboo?'

'Like a piece of bamboo, only black, with a hat and a funny smell, bamboo bamboo,' said Bu Hei.

'Just as I thought,' said Penny. 'Did you see what direction he went in, bamboo bamboo?'

'That way, bamboo bamboo,' said Bu Hei,
pointing to the door at the rear of the enclosure.

Penny started to head in that direction.

'Or maybe it was that way, bamboo bamboo,'
said Bu Hei, pointing to the front of the enclosure
where zoo visitors were jostling, desperately trying
to catch a glimpse of an absent albino panda.

Penny turned and went towards the crowd.

'Or on second thought, bamboo bamboo ...' said
Bu Hei.

But Penny ignored her. She'd had enough of
the silly pandas and their obsession with bamboo.
Being careful to avoid the clumps of bamboo that
the pandas were gathering and shoving into their
mouths, Penny slipped out of the enclosure and
into the crowd.

Chapter 6

A touch of home

Out in the crowd, Penny instantly regretted
her decision. She had landed in the single most
popular piece of zoo walkway, in front of the panda
enclosure.

Hundreds of pairs of feet shuffled backwards
and forwards, left and right, as their owners tried
to catch a glimpse of the albino panda. Since Black
Texta had only recently done his dirty work, none
of the zoo visitors knew there was no albino panda
to be seen, and they stubbornly continued looking
for it. Penny had to dodge from side to side, and
occasionally upend herself to avoid being trampled.

Just when she thought she could take it no more,
a voice to her right said, 'Psst! Over here!'

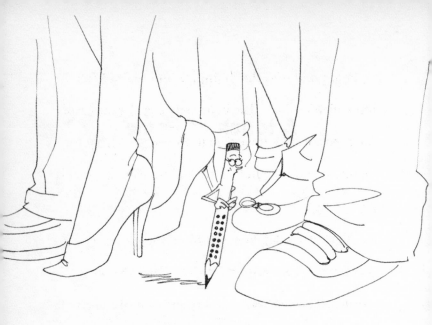

Penny turned and saw the outlet of a drainpipe. But instead of being just a round, black hole, it had eyes, a nose and whiskers.

'This way. Quickly – before you get crushed!'

The arch of a high-heeled shoe landed an inch above Penny's head, the toe and the heel either side of her. Penny wriggled out from underneath and rolled her way to the drainpipe, dodging a shoe here, a boot there, and even a clog.

When Penny got close to the drainpipe, the eyes and whiskers disappeared inside with a 'Follow me!'

Penny slid into the drainpipe and found herself immediately stuck. The bend between the outlet of the pipe and the downpipe itself was too sharp for Penny to bend around. There was no way she could get through it.

Penny waited, and a minute or so later there was the sound of scuffling feet and the eyes and whiskers reappeared.

'Sapristi Nyuckles! What are you doing? Don't tell me you fancy living in the outlet of this drainpipe for the rest of your life?'

'I don't actually,' said Penny, who, during her minutes of stuckness, had noticed that the drainpipe had a particularly unpleasant smell.

'Then what are you waiting for?' said the owner of the eyes and whiskers as he scuttled away again.

Penny tapped her toe impatiently until the pitter-patter of tiny paws returned.

'What's the matter?' asked the eyes and whiskers.

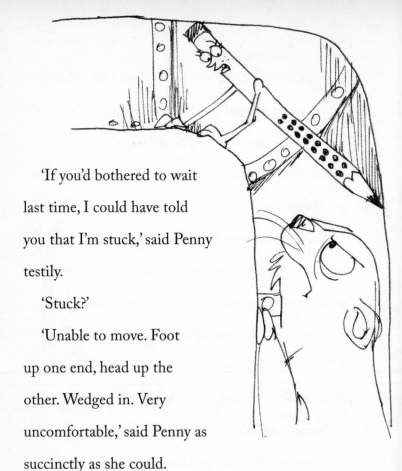

'If you'd bothered to wait last time, I could have told you that I'm stuck,' said Penny testily.

'Stuck?'

'Unable to move. Foot up one end, head up the other. Wedged in. Very uncomfortable,' said Penny as succinctly as she could.

'Why don't you just bend in the middle and shimmy on up after me?'

'Because I'm a pencil,' said Penny irritably. 'We don't shimmy and we certainly don't bend.'

'We? Is there more than one of you?'

'No. I mean pencils in general.'

The eyes and whiskers approached curiously. Penny could see that they belonged to an animal with a long, skinny body. The animal grabbed Penny's foot and tried to pull her round the bend in the pipe, making her even more stuck than before.

'It's no use,' said Penny, really not enjoying having her hip rammed into the bend of the pipe.

'We'll just have to go the other way then,' said the animal, giving Penny's foot a hefty shove.

Penny's head shot out of the pipe. For a moment she saw blue sky, then a heel appeared directly overhead, coming down rapidly. With less than an inch between her nose and the heel, Penny felt a tug on her own ankle as she was pulled to safety back inside the drainpipe.

'Are you all right?' asked the animal.

'I would be if someone didn't keep getting me wedged in stinky places and almost trodden on by zoo visitors,' grumbled Penny.

'Hey! The way I see it, I saved your life twice,' said the animal. 'What sort of stupid creature are you if you can't even bend around a drainpipe?'

'I've already told you, I'm a pencil,' said Penny through clenched teeth.

'What is that? Some kind of unbendy snake?'

'No. I'm not an animal,' said Penny. 'I'm a writing implement. Humans use me to put letters and numbers on things.'

'Why do they do that?' asked the whiskered animal curiously.

'So they can read it back to themselves or show it to other people,' said Penny.

'Oh,' said the animal. 'I don't know anything about reading.'

There was an awkward silence.

'So what kind of animal are you?' asked Penny, trying to change the subject.

'I'm a native Irish stoat!' said the animal proudly.

'Stoat … stoat …' said Penny, wracking her brain. 'Don't you mean a weasel?'

'DON'T use that word around me! There are no weasels in Ireland. We are all stoats. I would expect a learned pencil like yourself to have read that somewhere,' said the stoat in a huff.

'Er, right,' said Penny. 'I'm sorry, Mr Stoat …'

'Call me Milligan,' said the stoat.

'And my name's Penny,' said Penny.

'What brings you to the zoo, Penny?' asked Milligan.

'It's quite a long story, actually,' began Penny, telling Milligan about the safariddles, her meeting with the orangutans and the attack on Bu Hei.

'A texta factory, you say?' said Milligan.

'Yes,' said Penny.

'And they're planning to close the zoo?'

'Yes.'

'Well that doesn't help our cause at all!' said Milligan.

'Your cause?' asked Penny.

'To draw attention to the plight of the common Irish animal and raise their status to the same as exotic zoo imports,' recited Milligan.

'What?' said Penny.

'It might be easier if I show you. Come on, the coast's clear now.'

Milligan squeezed past Penny and poked his head out of the drainpipe.

'What are you waiting for?' asked Milligan, his tail disappearing out the hole.

Penny poked her head out cautiously. It had grown dark and there wasn't a single human about. The zoo had obviously closed for the evening. She followed Milligan along deserted pathways, past all types of animal enclosures, until they arrived at a tree with a very wide trunk and roots that poked up out of the ground.

Milligan leapt through the maze of roots before

arriving at a green wooden door with an orange shamrock painted on it. He *rat-a-tat-tatted* on the door and waited.

The door swung open and a little nose poked out, followed by several spines.

'Spike!' said the stoat, barging through the door and bowling over the hedgehog standing on the other side.

'Milligan!' said the hedgehog once he had picked himself up and dusted himself off.

'Crack open the good stuff! We have a visitor,' said Milligan, ushering Penny inside.

Penny looked around in amazement at the hollowed-out tree trunk that Spike and Milligan called home. It was like a cross between a pub and a souvenir shop. Leprechaun ornaments, gift sets of shamrock beer coasters and chipped pieces of Waterford crystal sat on every available surface. Any spare patch of wall was covered with signs

advertising Guinness,
or saying 'Free beer
tomorrow' or 'Fáilte'. It
was clear that neither
Spike nor Milligan could
read, as none of the signs
was hung the right way up, some being at an angle
and some completely upside down.

There was a kitchen in an alcove to the right and
a bedroom in an alcove to the left with two little
beds, which had matching bedspreads of the Irish
flag.

'Where did you get all this stuff?' asked Penny.

'Collected it,' said Spike proudly.

'Where from?'

'Under benches. Outside the toilets. Edge of the
playground. Loads of visitors leave bags behind,'
said Milligan.

Spike shook his head.

'All these tourists from abroad come to the zoo, laden with souvenirs of our fine country, yet there's no Irish animal section.'

'I once overheard an American tourist ask a keeper where the leprechaun exhibit was,' laughed Milligan.

'Is that what this is?' asked Penny. 'The Irish animal exhibit?'

'It isn't finished yet,' said Spike, bustling about. 'We have to build the window,' he continued, pointing to a surprisingly bare patch on the wall, with lines and measurements drawn on it in chalk.

'We're just waiting for the right piece of glass,' said Milligan.

'One of those glasses they have for sale at the Guinness factory should do,' said Spike.

'We just have to wait for a forgetful tourist to –'
Milligan was cut off by a high-pitched whinny.

'That sounded like Zelda. Let's go!' said Spike.

He bounded out of the door with amazing speed for a hedgehog, the stoat right behind him. Without knowing where she was going, Penny followed them out of the tree trunk and into the night.

Chapter 7

The missing zebra

Penny found keeping up with Spike and Milligan hard work. The sun had set long ago and it was pitch black. Penny had to rely on the pitter-patter of the eight paws in front of her to guide her way.

This was made all the harder by the grunts, roars and squeals coming from the zoo's other residents.

During a particularly loud roar, Penny didn't notice that the pitter-patter had stopped, and she ran straight into the back of Milligan, pushing him, in turn, into Spike.

'Ow!' cried Milligan, extracting several of Spike's spines out of his nose and various other parts of his body.

'Watch where you're going,' said Spike, rubbing the tiny bare patch of skin where his spines used to be.

Penny looked into the dark enclosure and couldn't see any animals. She squinted at the sign to try to read what sort of animal Zelda was, but it was too dark to make even a single letter out.

'Zelda! Zelda? Where are you?' called Spike.

A clippety-clop of hoofs grew louder and stopped very close to them.

'Zelda?' said Milligan.

'I'm right here,' said a female voice.

At that moment there was a loud clap of thunder and a bolt of lightning lit up the enclosure. Standing directly in front of Penny, Spike and Milligan was a black horse.

Spike and Milligan gasped as the black horse hung her head in shame.

'What's wrong with the horse?' Penny whispered to Milligan.

'Zelda's not a horse, she's a zebra,' said Milligan.

'But don't zebras have white stripes …?'

'I did until about an hour ago,' sobbed Zelda, 'until some weird-smelling guy stole them.'

'Stole them?' said Penny.

'Yeah. He took his hat off and sucked them all up, like a giant, bad-smelling vacuum cleaner. I look terrible!' continued Zelda with a sad whinny.

'Are you sure he sucked your stripes off?' asked Penny. 'He didn't just colour them in?'

'What's the difference?' whined Zelda. 'My stripes are gone aren't they?'

'Penny,' said Milligan in a low voice. 'Do you think it was the Black Texta bloke who attacked Bu Hei?'

'I'm sure of it,' said Penny.

'What am I going to do?' wailed Zelda. 'When the zoo visitors arrive tomorrow and see a black horse instead of a zebra, they're going to go home disappointed. Not to mention the lions ...'

'A pride of lions is coming to visit the zoo tomorrow?' asked Spike.

'No! The lions who live here,' continued Zelda. 'Now that I don't have my stripes for camouflage, they'll see me a mile off. It's just a matter of time before I become a tasty meal for them ...'

'Zelda,' began Milligan, 'we've told you before. The lions are safely locked in their enclosure with a moat, a twenty-foot-high reinforced concrete wall and an electric fence keeping them in.'

'It's the most fortified enclosure in the zoo,' added Spike.

'Apart from Herby's,' said Milligan.

He, Spike and Zelda all chuckled, just like the orangutans had at the mention of Herby.

'Who is this Herby?' asked Penny, her annoyance at being left out of the joke making her temporarily forget about Black Texta and Zelda's missing stripes.

'He's the Sumatran tiger,' said Spike, wiping tears from his eyes.

'I thought that tiger's name was Zultan,' said Penny, remembering the name from the keeper talk that morning.

'That's what the keepers call him,' chuckled Milligan.

'Then why do you call him Herby?' asked Penny.

'Because he's gone all New Age and discovered his inner vegan,' said Spike.

'Eh?' said Penny.

'You know. Vegan. He doesn't eat any animal products: no meat, no fish, no eggs, no dairy,' explained Milligan.

'No marshmallows, no jelly, no honey …' continued Spike.

'How many times have I told you?' interrupted Milligan. 'Not *all* marshmallows and jellies –'

'Don't forget ice-cream,' added Spike.

Milligan rolled his eyes.

'Not *all* marshmallows, jellies and ice-creams are made with vegan-unfriendly gelatine.'

'If you're quite finished,' said Penny impatiently.

'Yes. Well,' said Spike, giving Milligan an insulted look. 'The long and the short of it is that the Sumatran tiger is a complete herbivore, so we call him Herby for short.'

'He's also into aura cleansing and spiritual massage,' added Milligan.

'I don't trust his tarot card reading,' butted in Zelda. 'He didn't predict anything like this in my reading yesterday.'

'Speaking of Black Texta,' said Penny, 'we have to stop him before he attacks anybody else. Now, can you think of any other animals with black stripes or spots that Black Texta might want to colour in?'

'There's Herby,' said Spike, earning a chuckle from the others.

'Other than Herby,' said Penny.

'He might try to steal the white stripes off Stinky the skunk,' suggested Zelda.

'Or he could draw blotches on the polar bear

to turn him into some kind of arctic panda,' said Milligan.

'That sounds like a lot of ground to cover,' said Penny.

'But what about me?' asked Zelda.

There was another thunderclap and rain began to fall.

'I know!' said Spike. 'Just stand here in the rain and you'll wash clean!'

'No she won't,' said Penny. 'Black Texta's ink doesn't come out of anything. You need solvent to get rid of it.'

A lightning flash proved that Penny was right. Zelda was just as black as she had been before the rain started.

'Come on,' said Penny. 'If we're going to catch Black Texta we'll have to split up.'

Spike and Milligan opened their eyes in alarm.

'You mean … go searching for this guy, all on our own?' asked Spike.

'There are so many different animals to protect, we'll never get to them all in time unless we go separately,' argued Penny.

'Nu-uh,' said Spike, shaking his head.

'Well then,' said Penny with annoyance, 'you two pair up and I'll –'

'I don't think so! First sign of danger and this bloke curls up into a ball,' huffed Milligan, 'which is fine for some, but where does that leave me? I'll be coming with you.'

'Well I'm not going anywhere on my own,' said

Spike, crossing his arms over his chest.

Penny shook her head. 'Come on then, we'll all go together.'

Penny, Spike and Milligan spent the rest of the night searching the zoo for Black Texta. On quite a few occasions, Penny thought she caught a whiff of texta ink, but she didn't catch even a glimpse of her arch enemy. When they'd been all the way around the zoo and made sure that all the animals were the right colour, Penny insisted they go again, to yawns and protests from Spike and Milligan.

'There's no satisfying some people,' said Spike

when Penny suggested they go a third time just to be sure.

'Plus, the zoo's about to open!' said Milligan.

'I don't know about you,' said Spike, 'but I'm starving. How about we take a break and I'll cook up a grand breakfast – full Irish, of course.'

Penny opened her mouth to protest, but her words were drowned out by a big grumble from her tummy. She sheepishly followed Spike and Milligan back to the tree trunk.

She and Milligan discussed texta-trapping

strategies while Spike fried up a mound of eggs, bacon, black pudding, white pudding, tomatoes and beans.

Just as Spike was dishing up, a bell rang that sounded exactly like the bell at Ralph's school. Penny leaped up and stood to attention, much to the amusement of Spike and Milligan.

'What are you doing?' asked Spike, putting on oven gloves. 'You look like Milligan when he hears *Amhrán na bhFiann*!'

'Sorry,' said Penny, her cheeks flushing red. 'I thought it was the school bell.'

'Nope,' said Spike, opening the oven door and letting the delicious aroma of fresh brown bread fill the tree trunk. 'Just the oven timer. Grub's up!'

Penny, Milligan and Spike sat down to a hearty breakfast, unaware of the problems the other zoo animals were having with food from the moment the zoo visitors arrived.

Chapter 8

Do feed the animals

'Uh, Bob,' Fearful Fionnuala's voice crackled over the walkie-talkie, 'we've got another Code 3 at the aardvark enclosure.'

'Crikey!' said Bob. 'That's the eighth one this morning! What have those animals been eating?'

Bob hopped into his zoo buggy and sped over to the aardvark enclosure.

'There are traces of carrot, of course,' said Fearful Fionnuala, poking a gluggy puddle of aardvark vomit with a stick, 'and I think I can also identify peanut, fairy floss and that's definitely a chunk of hot dog.'

'No wonder the poor darling's been sick,' said Bob, stroking the ailing aardvark's snout. 'But how did all this junk food get into the animal's feed? And it's not just the aardvark. It's happening all over the zoo.'

Fearful Fionnuala peered into the aardvark's food trough.

'There's definitely no fairy floss or hot dogs in here. And on the red sign outside the enclosure it clearly says …' Fearful Fionnuala broke off.

'Do not feed the animals,' finished Bob, without looking up from the aardvark.

'No it doesn't,' said Fearful Fionnuala.

'What?' said Bob. 'Has the sign gone missing? Maybe the signs have fallen off the enclosures of the other sick animals –'

'The sign hasn't gone missing,' said Fearful Fionnuala. 'But it says *do* feed the animals.'

'Do *not* feed the animals,' corrected Bob.

'No,' said Fearful Fionnuala. 'Someone's blacked out the *not* so it says *do feed the animals.*'

Bob stopped stroking the aardvark's snout (much to the aardvark's dismay) and leaped up to look at the sign for himself.

'Blimey! You're right!' said Bob. 'Someone's vandalised the sign, so the visitors think we're encouraging them to feed the animals. But human food makes them sick. Quick! We'd better check the signs on all the other enclosures to make sure we don't get any more Code 3s!'

Bob and Fearful Fionnuala got into the zoo

buggy and sped around the zoo. Sure enough,
all the signs on the animal enclosures who had
suffered Code 3s that morning had been vandalised,
as well as a few more.

'Take the wheel!' cried Bob, leaping out of the
zoo buggy and across the fence into the crocodile
enclosure. He commando-rolled in front of the

open jaws of Max
the crocodile,
whisking a Mars bar
out of range in the nick of
time.

'A spewing crocodile is a sight
no one wants to see,' said Bob, breaking
the Mars bar in two and giving half to Fearful
Fionnuala once he'd scrambled out of the crocodile
enclosure. 'We'd better fix these signs on the
double.'

But no matter what sort of cleaner they used,
Bob and Fearful Fionnuala couldn't clean the black
ink off the signs.

'We'll just have to paint over it instead,'
said Bob, grabbing a can of red paint from the
maintenance shed to match the background colour
of the signs.

As they drove out of the shed, three men in

suits stepped onto the path. To avoid hitting them, Bob had to break so sharply that red paint flew out of the can, covering both himself and Fearful Fionnuala all down their fronts.

'And so you should be red-faced!' bellowed the Zoo Director, the man in the middle. He had fat cheeks and a big moustache that made him look like a walrus.

Before Bob or Fearful Fionnuala had a chance to apologise, the Zoo Director carried on, 'This place is a disgrace! Animals vomiting all over the place, customers thinking it's okay to give popcorn to a rhinoceros

and having their shirts sprayed with rhino vomit … The dry cleaning bill from this morning's little fiasco will be enough to make us broke. We have no choice but to sell now.'

The fat, balding man on the right rubbed his hands together with glee. As the Mayor, he would be receiving a nice cut from the sale of the zoo. The tall man on the left, with black hair that was so shiny and smooth it looked like a plastic helmet, sneered in delight.

A secretary with thick, black-rimmed glasses bustled up out of nowhere, passing a sheet of paper with Contract of Sale written across the top in big, bold letters.

'Allow me,' said the Mayor, pulling a pen out of his top pocket and offering it to the Zoo Director.

'No!' cried a female voice, as a figure flew in between the Mayor and the Zoo Director, snatching the pen away. It was Fearful Fionnuala.

Everyone was shocked, not least of all Fearful Fionnuala who became her normal fearful self and started trembling.

'I … I … just meant … what about the … the … animals?'

'It's all there in the fine print at the end,' said the Mayor, taking the pen out of Fearful Fionnuala's hand and giving it back to the Zoo Director.

'I really shouldn't sign this until I've read it,' said the Zoo Director, holding the pen above the contract. 'I left my glasses back in the office. Where exactly does it say you'll be sending the animals?'

'Circuses mainly,' said the tall man, licking his lips at the sight of the pen above the contract.

'What?' cried Bob. 'An aardvark in the circus? What's it going to do? Walk the tightrope?'

'Oh, you'd be surprised by what ringmasters can get animals to do these days,' said the tall man. 'It's merely a question of … encouragement.'

'No. Absolutely not,' said Bob. 'None of these animals are joining any circus.'

'In that case,' said the tall man, 'there are a number of research labs who've expressed an interest in taking the animals. They normally have such difficulty laying their hands on … *exotic* species for their experiments.'

Bob's eyes widened in horror and he started shaking even more than Fearful Fionnuala.

'There has to be another way,' said Bob quietly.

A drop of ink dangled from the end of the pen, threatening to spill onto the contract. The tall man's eyes widened as the droplet hovered closer and closer to the paper.

'I can't do it,' said the Zoo Director suddenly, handing the contract back to the Mayor's secretary.

The drop of ink fell harmlessly to the ground.

The Mayor's face turned red and a tiny puff of smoke came out of each ear.

The tall man's expression turned steely.

'This is a once-only offer,' he spat. 'Our terms next time will not be so generous.'

'I won't sign any contract,' said the Zoo Director quietly, 'until we find homes where all the animals will be happy.'

Before anyone else could say anything, the cashier from the front gate of the zoo ran up, chased by an angry mob.

'Mr Director, Sir,' said the cashier, quite out of breath. 'These people all want their money back –'

'We paid to see an albino panda, but there isn't one. That's false advertising!' complained one.

'The zebra's not there,' whinged another.

'If I'd known I was going to be sprayed with

walrus vomit, I would have stayed home,' growled another.

'This is your last chance,' said the tall man, snatching the contract from the secretary and thrusting it under the Zoo Director's nose.

'As you can see,' said the Director calmly, 'I have urgent matters to attend to.'

And with that, he, Bob and Fearful Fionnuala turned their backs on the Mayor and the tall man, who grimaced after them.

Chapter 9

Petition

'Penny! Penny! Wake up!'

Snoozily, Penny opened one eye, to see a leprechaun dancing around a familiar, whiskered face. She rubbed her eyes and shook her head. When she opened them again, she realised that Milligan was standing in front of a clock with a leprechaun attached to the second hand.

'The time for action has come,' said Milligan gravely.

'Is it Black Texta? Is he here?' asked Penny, leaping out of bed and looking around the tree trunk.

'Worse,' said Spike.

'Worse?' exclaimed Penny.

'While we were running round the zoo last night like headless chickens, looking for Black Texta inside all the enclosures, he was one step ahead of us,' continued Spike.

'Where was he?' asked Penny.

'Outside the enclosures,' said Milligan. 'Changing the signs.'

'Which signs?'

'The "Do not feed the animals" signs,' said Spike. 'People have been throwing human food at the animals all morning.'

'And the animals have thrown it up straight back at them,' added Milligan.

'Have you any idea what happens when a penguin eats a tomato sandwich?' asked Spike.

'Er, no,' said Penny.

128

'Trust me, it isn't pretty,' said Milligan,
shuddering at the thought.

'None of it's pretty,' said Spike. 'And we're
wasting time sitting around just talking about it.
Let's get out there and help!'

Penny and Milligan followed Spike out of the tree trunk and through the zoo, dodging puddle after puddle of animal vomit that decorated the pathways. The usual tweets, roars and warbles were replaced by groans, heaves and splatters.

'Who would have thought that a pygmy shrew could projectile vomit this much this far!' said Milligan, tiptoeing around a huge mound of recycled liquorice allsorts and, of course, carrot.

'Incoming!' cried Spike, pushing Penny out of the way just as a shower of gummy bears, ice-cream and carrot gushed out of a hippopotamus' mouth, landing exactly where Penny had been one second earlier.

'That was a big one!' said Penny.

'Speaking of big,' said Milligan, 'just how big is this Black Texta bloke? Three feet? Six feet?'

'Probably about this much taller than me,' said Penny, reaching her arm above her head as high as it would go.

'Then how does he do it?' asked Milligan
thoughtfully.

'He just takes his cap off and –' began Penny.

'No. I mean … how does he do *all* of it? There
must be over one hundred animals here, so there
are one hundred signs to colour in. Plus he's already
attacked Bu Hei and Zelda. He's got to run out of
ink some time,' reasoned Milligan.

131

'Unless …' said Penny. 'Of course!'

'Of course what?' said Spike and Milligan together.

'The ink tanks! The ones by the panda enclosure. He's refilling himself whenever he runs out of ink!' said Penny.

'No wonder Bu Hei was the first victim,' said Spike, shaking his head.

'So you're saying that instead of running out of ink, Black Texta has a limitless supply for carrying out his dirty deeds?' said Milligan.

Penny nodded.

'We can't fight that,' said Spike.

'Oh, don't be so spineless,' said Milligan. 'We don't shy away from the enemy just because they're bigger and stronger than us!'

'Shh!' whispered Penny. 'Listen.'

Spike and Milligan stood silent for a moment.

'I don't hear anything,' said Milligan.

'Neither do I,' said Penny. 'The vomiting's stopped.'

Not a single retch, squelch or splatter could be heard.

'What's that?' said Milligan, cocking his head.

'What's what?' asked Penny.

'Can't you hear it? It's coming from over there,' said Spike pointing to a curve in the path.

'I still can't hear …' began Penny.

'It sounds a bit like rain,' said Spike, as the noise grew louder.

'Or a river in flood,' said Milligan, going over to investigate the source of the noise, which was now thunderous.

No sooner had Milligan's tail disappeared around the corner, than his whiskers reappeared, and he was in an awful hurry.

'Spew avalanche! Run!' cried Milligan as he hurtled past Spike and Penny.

Spike curled up into a ball and rolled after Milligan.

Penny watched in horror as a high pressure hose drove dried animal vomit down the path around the corner.

'Stop!' cried a voice, as Penny felt herself scooped up by a trembling hand. It was Fearful Fionnuala.

'We can't wash this down the recycling drain!'

Fearful Fionnuala held Penny up to show Bob.

'That was a close call,' said Bob, examining Penny. 'Not that our organic refuse recycle plant is all that useful any more with the zoo closing …'

Both Bob and Fearful Fionnuala's walkie-talkies crackled at the same time.

'When you two are done cleaning the paths,' said the Zoo Director's voice, 'come to my office.'

'Yes sir,' said Bob, popping Penny in his top pocket before turning the hose back on.

* * *

When Bob, Fearful Fionnuala and Penny arrived in the Zoo Director's office, the Director was in a terrible state.

'What are we going to do about

this mess?' he asked.

'Sir, we've mucked out all the enclosures and pressure hosed the paths …' began Bob.

'I don't mean that mess, I mean this mess! The zoo closing. How can we save the animals?'

'I've got an idea,' said Fearful Fionnuala.

Both Bob and the Zoo Director looked at her.

'While I was picking up pavement pizza,' said Fearful Fionnuala, blushing, 'I thought we could maybe petition the Mayor.'

'Petition him?' said the Zoo Director.

'You know, collect lots of signatures from happy zoo visitors,' said Fearful Fionnuala.

'How's that going to help?' asked the Zoo Director.

'When the Mayor sees how popular the zoo is, he'll realise how *un*popular he'll be if he lets it close,' said Fearful Fionnuala.

'Cor! That's brilliant!' said Bob.

'There's only one problem,' said the Zoo Director. 'After this morning's feeding fiasco, where are we going to find happy zoo visitors to sign the petition?'

'Easy,' said Fearful Fionnuala. 'The people who came to the zoo yesterday. Kids are great at getting people to buy raffle tickets and sponsor them in readathons and things. How easy would it be for that class from Finbarr Primary to get signatures from everybody? They're free!'

'I'm still not convinced,' said the Zoo Director, looking doubtful. 'After all, a petition is only words on paper. What use is that?'

'Harumph!' huffed Penny angrily from Bob's top pocket, but, being human, the other three occupants of the room couldn't hear her.

'Lots of use!' said Fearful Fionnuala. 'In fact the only thing the Mayor really cares about.'

'That's not true,' said the Zoo Director. 'He cares about votes and how much money's in his bank account.'

'Exactly,' said Fearful Fionnuala, getting less and less fearful by the minute. 'Votes are just words on paper, the balance of his bank account is just numbers on paper. If we can get big numbers of signatures on paper, then he'll care,' Fearful Fionnuala finished, crossing her arms and nodding her head defiantly.

A slow smile crept across the Zoo Director's face.

'Fionnuala, you're absolutely right,' he said. 'If you pull this off, I'll promote you to Head Keeper.'

'Harumph!' huffed Bob.

'That's *equal* Head Keeper,' said the Zoo Director. 'Well? What are you waiting for? We won't collect any signatures by standing around here all day.'

Bob and Fearful Fionnuala ran out of the Zoo Director's office, colliding in the doorway. The bump knocked Penny out of Bob's pocket.

'Nooooo …!' she cried, as she toppled to the concrete below with her eyes shut tight.

But instead of landing on the hard concrete and being smashed to pieces, she landed toe first in something warm and soft.

'Ow! Watch where you're sticking that sharp point!' said a familiar voice.

Penny opened her eyes and found herself in the middle of a sea of spines.

'Spike?' she said.

'Would you mind removing your point from my skin? It's rather sharp,' said Spike.

'Now you know what it feels like,' said Milligan, as Penny carefully extracted herself from Spike's back.

'What are you two doing here?'

asked Penny.

'Rescuing you, of course,' said Milligan.

'Speak for yourself,' said Spike, rubbing the little hole in his back.

'What intelligence have you gathered?' asked Milligan.

'Well, they're doing a petition to stop the zoo from closing,' said Penny.

'What's a petition?' asked Spike.

Penny quickly explained.

'If it works, we could get all the animals to sign a petition for us to get an Irish animal exhibit!' said Milligan enthusiastically. 'Let's call a general meeting to spread the good news.'

* * *

At six o'clock that evening, just after closing time, Spike and Milligan held a general meeting of all the animals in the zoo. None of the animals had

ever heard of a petition before, and Penny had to explain what it was and how they expected it to work. Many of the animals doubted that it would work, but the pandas, on the other hand, were quite confident.

'How do we sign, bamboo bamboo?' asked Bu Hei's mother.

A smile spread across Penny's face.

'Exactly,' she said.

Chapter 10

The truth about Bert

Mack was struggling to help Ralph with his
Maths lesson when there was a knock on the
classroom door. Mrs Sword looked at the clock
and smiled.

'Class, pencils down. We have a visitor.'

All the children put their pencils
down immediately and watched
Mrs Sword walk to the door.

'Crikey! It's Bob from the zoo!'
said Ralph as Mrs Sword opened
the door.

'Hello kids,' said Bob. 'Did
you all enjoy your trip to the zoo
yesterday?'

'Yeeeeeeeeeeeeeeeees,' chorused the class.

'Would you like to visit the animals again?' asked Bob.

'Yeeeeeeeeeeeeeeeees,' chorused the class with even more enthusiasm.

'Then the animals are going to need your help,' said Bob.

'Why?' asked Malcolm.

145

'Because the Mayor is trying to sell the zoo to a man who's going to build a texta factory in its place.'

'No!' chorused the class in outrage – apart from Ralph and Sarah, who gave each other a knowing nod.

'What will happen to the animals?' asked Ciara.

'I'm not exactly sure …' began Bob.

'I'll adopt the elephant!' offered Seán.

'And I'd like a seal,' said Lucy.

'If only it were that easy,' said Bob. 'Now I'm sure you'd all take good care of the animals if you were to adopt them …'

The whole class nodded enthusiastically, with Bert the most enthusiastic of all.

'… but you need a special licence and special training to keep exotic animals, which is why they're only in zoos,' continued Bob. 'To keep them in our zoo, we need your help. We've started a petition to show the Mayor how many people are against

the zoo closing. And we need signature collectors.
Would anyone like to volunteer to collect signatures
to save the animals?'

Thirty hands shot straight into the air.

'Excellent,' said Bob, handing out sheets of
paper to everyone with plenty of room for lots of
signatures.

'I'll take two,' said Sarah as Bob got to her
desk.

'I'll take ten,' said Bert.

'Bert, this is serious,' said Sarah. 'The animals
need our help.'

'Which is why I'm going to get as many signatures as possible,' said Bert.

'As if,' said Sarah under her breath. She still hadn't forgiven Bert for getting to the Octopus, Seals, Antelope, Flamingo, Alpaca, Rhinoceros and Indian elephant before her and being the first to work out the mystery phrase 'HAPPY ZOO SAFARI'.

'He might be serious,' said Ralph. 'He did know the difference between the octopus and the chimpala.'

'That was okapi and impala, Nolan,' said Bert in his usual scornful tone, 'but thanks for sticking up for me,' he added softly.

When the bell rang, instead of being disappointed that school was over, Sarah was excited about going signature-collecting.

'I don't care if I've got two sheets and Bert's got ten sheets,' said Sarah, 'I'm going to get the most signatures. I'll use the back of the page if I have to.'

'Don't forget to get your parents' permission before you go traipsing around the neighbourhood,' said Mrs Sword as the children hurried out of the classroom.

Ralph's mother was only too happy for Ralph to collect signatures to save the zoo. Sarah's grandmother also thought it was a worthwhile cause, but only let Sarah go on the condition that she and Ralph stick together and were home before dark.

'Come on!' said Sarah. 'We've only got a couple of hours. You take that side of the street and I'll take this side!'

Ralph and Sarah went from house to house, ringing on doorbells and collecting signatures. Everyone they spoke to signed the petition straight away and even Sarah's second sheet was filling up fast.

'One more street should do it,' said Sarah as they got to the corner of Dark Street.

'Shouldn't we go on to the next street?' asked Ralph, not liking the look of the houses on Dark Street at all.

'Don't tell me you're scared,' said Sarah.

Ralph looked down Dark Street and tried not to shiver, wishing that Sarah's competitive streak wouldn't get in the way of her common sense. Dark Street looked pretty dangerous and definitely skippable as far as Ralph was concerned.

'Come on,' said Sarah. 'No one else from school will have gone down here.'

'No one else from school has a death wish like you do,' muttered Ralph, reluctantly following Sarah through the gate of the first house.

They trudged up the long, overgrown driveway and rang the buzzer. A tuneless bell donged from the depths of the house. Ralph thought he saw a

dusty curtain in the upstairs window move, but
nobody came to the door.

'Let's go,' said Ralph.

'You give up too easily,' said Sarah, pressing the
doorbell again and tapping her foot impatiently.

'No one's coming,' said Ralph. 'Let's get out of
here.'

Sarah followed Ralph back out onto Dark Street. The same thing happened at the next house, and the one after that.

'Look, nobody's home in this street. Can we get out of here now?' pleaded Ralph.

'Let's try this house,' said Sarah.

The house they had come to was different from all the others. The lawn was so neatly trimmed that it looked like the blades of grass were lined up like soldiers. The house itself was painted black, and the painting was done so smoothly that the walls glistened as though they were still wet.

'I've got a bad feeling about this,' said Ralph.

'What's the problem?' said Sarah, marching up to the front door and ringing the bell loudly. She sized up the house and turned back to Ralph. 'It's the best house on the street.'

Sarah turned back towards the house and gasped. The front door had swung open. A tall man in a black suit, with black hair so shiny and smooth it looked like a plastic helmet, was standing silently in the doorway. A faint inky smell flowed out of the house.

'Oh, hello,' said Sarah. 'We're here on behalf of the animals at Kilknock Zoo ...'

At that point the tall man's nostrils flared so wide that Ralph worried the man would suck Sarah right up them when he breathed in.

'I don't know if you're aware that the Mayor is planning to sell the zoo and turn it into a texta factory ...' continued Sarah.

The man's eyes narrowed into such small slits that

Ralph thought he looked like a snake, and an angry, poisonous one at that.

'... but we're putting a petition to the Mayor to stop the sale,' finished Sarah, holding up the petition proudly at the end of her spiel.

'Are you really?' said the man in a deep, sinister voice.

'Y-yes we are ...' said Sarah, noticing for the first time that the man was not smiling.

'And how many signatures have you got?' asked the man.

'Fifty-seven,' said Sarah proudly. 'Would you care to make it fifty-eight?'

'I most certainly wouldn't ...' began the man, extremely angrily. Then his face changed '... want to disappoint you,' he finished, reaching for the petition.

'Noooooooooooooooooo!'

Something shot past Ralph, between Sarah

and the man, and grabbed the petition. To Ralph's surprise it was a boy he knew only too well.

'Bert! What are you doing?' cried Sarah, trying to snatch the petition away from him.

'Saving the animals,' said Bert, holding the petition behind his back and stepping out of the man's reach.

'Give that back! He was about to sign it,' said Sarah.

'He was about to tear it up!' said Bert. 'Don't you know who he is?'

Sarah and Ralph looked from Bert to the man and back again.

'He's Troy Cettafax,' said Bert. 'He's the one who wants to build the texta factory!'

Ralph and Sarah gasped.

Mr Cettafax narrowed his eyes even further at Bert. Ralph almost expected him to grow fangs and spit venom. Grabbing Sarah in one hand and Bert in the other, Ralph ran down the path, dragging the others to safety.

Once down the street and around the corner, Ralph stopped running. The children collapsed on the footpath and caught their breath.

'Bert,' said Sarah, 'how did you know who Troy Cettafax is? And where he lives?'

Bert cleared his throat.

'I looked it up on the internet,' he said.

'Why?' asked Ralph.

Bert looked uncomfortable.

'I couldn't let the animals go homeless. I had to do something,' said Bert.

'I didn't know you liked animals so much,' said Sarah.

'Yeah, well, animals are easier to get on with than people,' admitted Bert. He turned to Ralph. 'Thanks for getting us out of there when you did. Who knows what Troy Cettafax would have done

if he had got hold of us. Maybe put us in a research lab like his plans for the animals.'

'Thanks for showing up when you did,' said Ralph, 'otherwise our whole petition would have been destroyed.'

The three children looked at each other uneasily. They weren't used to being on the same side.

'I guess neither of you feel like wagging school tomorrow morning and dropping these off at the zoo?' asked Bert.

Ralph looked at Sarah, who was scowling at Bert.

'Now that's where you're wrong, Bert,' said Sarah finally. 'We'd love to come.'

Chapter 11

Showdown

'Ow! Is this really necessary?' squealed Spike as Penny and then Milligan plucked a spine each out of Spike's coat.

'We need something sharp to whittle the bamboo into textas,' said Penny, pulling an extra spine out.

'Ow! Why not just get the pandas to nibble them down to the right shape?' complained Spike, rubbing the spots in his coat where the recently plucked spines used to be.

'We tried that, remember?' said Penny. 'But they just kept on eating.'

'How many of these do we need anyway?' asked Milligan, looking at the store of bamboo in the corner.

'Maybe just one. But it wouldn't hurt to have a spare or two,' said Penny, whittling one end of a stick of bamboo into a fine point.

'I don't see why we're bothering,' said Spike, accidentally stabbing himself with his own spine whilst whittling another stick of bamboo. 'Hey! These are sharp!'

'Isn't that the *point*?' said Milligan.

Spike and Milligan both burst out laughing.

'You two, be serious!' scolded Penny. 'We need to get this done quickly.'

Spike and Milligan looked at each other like

naughty schoolboys who'd been told off by the teacher, then the three of them continued whittling in silence.

'Good,' said Penny once they'd finished. 'Now we need something for the wick.'

'The wick? We're making candles?' said Spike. 'I thought we were making –'

'Candles aren't the only things that have wicks,' said Penny, looking around the room for suitable wick-making material. 'I need something absorbent …'

Her eyes fell on the bedspreads. Penny's face lit up.

Spike and Milligan turned to see what Penny was looking at, then shook their heads vigorously, running between Penny and the bedspreads.

'You can't,' said Milligan, backing up as Penny came towards them.

'Destroying the Irish flag is the highest act of treason,' said Spike, taking a step backwards.

'Not to mention unpatriotic,' added Milligan, shuffling back.

'It's detrimental to our cause,' said Spike, dropping back another step.

'It'll be detrimental to all the animals in the zoo – not just the Irish ones – if the zoo gets turned into a texta factory,' said Penny, still moving towards the stoat and the hedgehog.

Spike and Milligan had backed up so far that with the next step backwards they toppled onto their beds.

'Hand 'em over,' said Penny.

Spike and Milligan shook their heads.

'Now!' said Penny.

Spike and Milligan looked at each other.

'You go first,' said Milligan gallantly.

'Oh, I couldn't possibly,' said Spike. 'You go.'

'No, no,' said Milligan. 'I insist.'

'Why don't you go together?' said Penny, grabbing a corner of each bedspread and whipping them out from under Spike and Milligan, like a magician pulling a tablecloth off a fully laid table.

Spike and Milligan watched with tears in their eyes, humming the Irish anthem, as Penny tore the bedspreads into ribbons and stuffed them into the whittled bamboo.

'This is a very honourable sacrifice you've made,' said Penny once she'd finished. 'Now stop blubbering and follow me.'

Penny passed Spike and Milligan a stuffed bamboo each and led the way to the ink tanks

outside the panda enclosure.

'Now, we have to be very careful,' said Penny, turning around to face Spike and Milligan. 'Black Texta could be lurking anywhere …'

'He could indeed,' said a familiar, sinister voice behind her.

Penny felt a chill go down her spine. Spike curled up into a little ball and Milligan started shaking even more than Fearful Fionnuala.

Frightened of what Black Texta would look like this time round, Penny turned slowly. Black Texta was his ugliest yet. His body was no longer straight, but twisted and warped. Large welts and boils covered his casing, and there were pale grey blotches all over it. Despite all that, the sneer on his contorted face was the same as always.

'We meet again, Penny Pencil,' said Black Texta.

'So we do, Black-and-Grey Polka-Dot Texta,' said Penny with all the bravery she could muster.

'Ha ha ha,' laughed Black Texta mirthlessly. 'Always the clever one, aren't we? Trying to show off in front of your new friends, pom-pom and weasel?'

'Hey!' began Milligan, his pride getting the better of his fear. 'I am not a wea –'

'Did I give you permission to speak?' bellowed
Black Texta.

'N-n-no, Sir,' squeaked Milligan.

'That's better,' said Black Texta, giving Milligan
an icy stare before turning his attention back to
Penny. 'Now what would you be doing here of all
places, Ms Penny Pencil?'

'I could ask you the same question,' said Penny.
'But I know the answer already.'

'Do you?' said Black Texta, looking amused.

'Yes. You're refilling yourself with ink from those tanks over there.'

'Am I?' said Black Texta, the trace of a smile on his lips. Like lightning Black Texta shot out an arm and wrenched the bamboo out of Penny's hand. 'It would appear you have been stealing from the panda enclosure.' He examined the bamboo more closely. 'This isn't ordinary bamboo. If I didn't know better, I'd say you were making textas.'

Penny shuffled uncomfortably on her foot.

'How ironic that we should be here for the same purpose,' laughed Black Texta.

'I hardly think so,' said Penny. 'We're making textas to keep the zoo open, rather than waiting for it to shut before building an evil empire.'

'Uh, Penny …' began Milligan.

'Not now,' hissed Penny.

'Making textas,' laughed Black Texta. 'I never thought I'd see the day …'

'Pen-neeeee …' began Spike.

'I said not now,' said Penny.

'Tell you what,' said Black Texta, 'how about we join forces?'

'Never,' said Penny.

'Writing implements against animals. We'd make a great team.'

'No thank you,' said Penny. 'I've got my own team.'

'And I have mine,' said Black Texta, his eyes narrowing. 'Men!'

Only then did Penny notice the hundred or so black textas closing in from all directions.

'Where did they come from?' Penny said to Spike and Milligan out of the corner of her mouth.

'They've been there the whole time!' squeaked Spike.

'Why didn't you tell me?'

Despite the seriousness of the situation, Spike and Milligan rolled their eyes at each other.

'As you can see,' said Black Texta, 'I'm not waiting for the zoo to shut before building my evil empire.'

The textas pulled their lids off and tossed them in a heap at the bottom of the ink tanks before advancing on Penny and the others. Penny and Milligan huddled as close to Spike as they could without skewering themselves on his spines.

'How delicious!' laughed Black Texta. 'Death by hedgehog!'

'Rrrrroaaaar!'

A swirl of orange and black flew through the air, landing with four paws surrounding Penny, Spike and Milligan. An orange and black tail flicked left and right, knocking away the advancing black textas. One by one each texta was whacked unconscious against the side of an ink tank. Within seconds there was only one left.

'What's wrong, Black Texta?' sneered the

owner of the orange and black tail. 'Too much of a scaredy-cat to take me on?'

Black Texta narrowed his eyes and pulled off his lid, tossing it on the pile of other texta lids. He bent his head forward and charged.

At the same instant the orange and black paws lifted off the ground as their owner leapt at Black Texta. Only then did Penny realise that they belonged to a tiger.

'Is that …?' began Penny as tiger and texta hurtled towards each other.

'Yep. That's Herby,' said Spike, unfurling to watch the action.

'But isn't he …?' began Penny again as Herby and Black Texta collided.

Black Texta drew a black streak across Herby's left side from shoulder to haunch. He was so busy gloating at having got the first strike, he didn't see the orange and black tail lash at him.

Herby's tail hit Black Texta square between the eyes. Black Texta smashed into a tank, making a dent so large it punctured the side. Dazed, Black Texta slid to the ground below, liquid from the hole in the tank dripping onto him.

'He's fallen in the water!' cried Spike and Milligan together.

Black Texta sneered. 'Not water, ink. With every second I'm getting stronger as more ink drips onto me.'

'Are you?' asked Penny.

Black Texta closed his eyes and leaned back. He opened his mouth and let the liquid flow down his throat. After two drops he sat up, coughing and spluttering.

'This … this isn't ink!' he wheezed.

Only then did he bother to read the label on the tank. It was one word: S-O-L-V-E-N-T.

'Solvent!' cried Black Texta weakly. 'That's poison

for textas! Help me …'

Before their eyes, Black Texta melted away in the pool of solvent that had formed below the tank. Penny, Spike, Milligan and Herby trotted over for a closer look. All they could see were their own reflections in the rippling surface of the pool.

'I wonder what he'll come back as in his next life?' mused Herby out loud.

'You mean … he's not finished this time either?' spluttered Penny, looking at the pool fearfully as though she expected Black Texta to rise out of it.

174

'He'll be back *again*?'

'Sure,' said Herby. 'Everyone comes back to life if you believe in reincarnation like I do. In his next life I expect he'll come back as something really low on the food chain, like a dung beetle.'

Penny giggled at the thought of Black Texta with wings and six legs, sitting on a pile of dung.

'Hey,' said Milligan. 'I thought you were a pacifist, Herby.'

'I am,' said the tiger.

'Then what was all that texta carnage about?' asked Spike.

'Karma,' said Herby simply. 'I just closed my eyes and flicked my tail. I wasn't aiming for any particular texta, or any particular tank. Karma took care of the rest.'

And with that, Herby headed off, swishing his tail behind him. When he got to his enclosure, he sat on his haunches, crossed his hind legs, rested his front paws on his knees and chanted 'Om' over and over again. Within a few minutes he rose slowly off the ground, floated over the fence of his enclosure and lightly touched down under a Bodhi tree.

'Now *that* is one cool cat,' said Spike.

Chapter 12

Karma restored

'Well,' said Penny, 'now that Black Texta's been taken care of I guess I'll –'

'You'll do no such thing,' said Milligan. 'Need I remind you that we're in the middle of an operation? We have textas to make and signatures to collect, and thanks to this little ambush, very little time to do it in. Move, move, move!'

Spike drilled a little hole in the bottom of an ink tank and Penny held the bamboo textas underneath to fill them up with ink. But she didn't fill all three. She dipped the last one in the pool of solvent instead.

'What's that for?' asked Milligan.

'You'll see,' said Penny with a mysterious smile.

Carrying a texta each, they crept through the zoo to the zebra enclosure.

'Zelda!' called Spike.

He was answered by a clip-clop and a strange creaking sound.

'Sapristi yakamakaka!' said Milligan. 'Would you look at the size of it!'

Zelda was hitched up to a cart with a huge roll of paper on it.

'I got the biggest roll of paper I could find. We

may be low down the food chain, but we zebras can be pretty resourceful you know,' said Zelda.

'That's perfect, Zelda,' said Penny. 'Even the elephants' signatures will fit easily on that.'

The four of them went around the zoo from enclosure to enclosure, getting all the animals to sign the petition. Finally they made it back to the panda enclosure. Penny had insisted on saving the pandas until last.

'And a lucky thing too!' said Milligan, scolding Bu Hei's mother for eating the first bamboo texta – 'What's this weird filling in the centre, bamboo bamboo?' – and watching the other pandas closely to make sure they didn't do the same.

'You're the lucky last, Bu Hei,' said Penny, as the baby panda was the last to sign her name on the petition.

'Does that mean I can eat the texta, bamboo bamboo?' asked Bu Hei.

'Go for it!' said Penny.

'What about that one, bamboo bamboo?' asked Bu Hei with her mouth full, pointing to the texta with solvent in it.

'Ah,' said Penny. 'Zelda, go and stand next to Bu
Hei and close your eyes. You too, Bu Hei. Now this
may tickle a little …'

Penny scribbled all over Bu Hei and Zelda with
the solvent texta. Gradually the black ink started
to dissolve. When Penny had finished, instead of a
regular panda and a black horse, there was a zebra
and an albino panda standing in front of her.

'Yay!' cried Zelda. 'I look like me again. Now I'll be able to hide from the lions.'

Unlike Zelda, Bu Hei was anything but happy.

'What's wrong, Bu Hei?' asked Penny.

'I liked looking like all the other pandas, bamboo bamboo,' said Bu Hei. 'Now all those people are going to come back and point at me, bamboo bamboo.'

'But that's a good thing,' said Penny. 'Those people come to the zoo specially to see you. You're the star attraction!'

'I am, bamboo bamboo?' said Bu Hei, brightening.

'Definitely,' said Penny.

'Time's marching on,' said Milligan. 'In case you hadn't noticed, the sun's up, and we have to get this petition to the Director before the zoo opens.'

Penny, Spike and Milligan hopped on the back of the cart with the petition, and waved goodbye to the pandas as Zelda pulled them to the Director's office. They unloaded the petition, then Zelda hurried back to her enclosure, while Penny, Spike and Milligan hid behind a convenient flower pot to watch what the Director would do when he saw the petition.

At one minute before opening time, the Zoo Director arrived at his office. He muttered to himself as he unlocked the door, and tripped over the petition that he hadn't seen lying on the mat outside.

He picked it up, fished his glasses out of his pocket, and began to read.

'Extraordinary!' he said, looking around the zoo. 'Absolutely extraordinary!'

At one minute after opening time Bob, Fearful Fionnuala and three children came running along the path and knocked on the door of the Director's office.

'It's Ralph!' squeaked Penny. 'My owner! He's here!'

'Which one is he? The big one or the freckly one?' asked Spike.

'The freckly one,' said Penny. 'The girl is Sarah, Ralph's best friend. But I don't know what the big one's doing here. He's Bert the Bully, and he and Ralph are enemies.'

'You mean he's the Black Texta of the kid world?' asked Milligan.

'That's one way of putting it,' said Penny.

The Zoo Director opened the door with a look of puzzlement on his face.

'Sir,' said Bob excitedly. 'These children have been out collecting signatures for the petition to the Mayor and got over three hundred in one afternoon.'

'Is that so?' said the Director, rubbing his chin thoughtfully.

'Once we show this to the Mayor and he sees how many votes he'll lose, there's no way he'll close the zoo,' said Fearful Fionnuala.

'Here's your chance to find out,' said the Zoo Director, looking past the keepers and children.

Two grim men in suits were coming along the path: the Mayor and Troy Cettafax.

When Troy Cettafax saw the children, his face grew even grimmer.

'We've come for your signature,' said the Mayor, thrusting a new contract at the Zoo Director. 'And this time we're not leaving without it.'

Troy Cettafax merely sneered.

'I rather think you will be,' said the Director, handing the children's petition to the Mayor.

'What's this?' asked the Mayor.

'A petition to keep the zoo open,' said the Zoo Director. 'Our young friends over there obtained three hundred signatures last night. That translates to a lot of lost votes, especially with an election around the corner.'

'Don't take any notice, Mayor,' said Troy

Cettafax. 'It's all a hoax. These young delinquents probably scrawled all the so-called signatures themselves. And besides, they should be in school.'

'No we shouldn't,' said Sarah haughtily. 'Our guardians signed permission slips for us to take the morning off school and deliver the petitions to the zoo.'

'And we'd hardly bother carrying our school bags if we were taking the whole day off,' added Bert.

'Grrrr,' grrrred Troy Cettafax.

'Would you still like me to sign the contract?' the Zoo Director asked the Mayor, his pen poised over the paper.

'Now, now, we shouldn't do anything hasty,' said the Mayor, hastily snatching the contract from the Zoo Director and tearing it up. 'I'm sorry, Mr Cettafax, but clearly this zoo and the welfare of its animals is more important to the people of this town than a texta factory.'

'Yay!' cried Ralph, Sarah and Bert, jumping up and down and hugging each other.

Bob and Fearful Fionnuala gave each other a high five, while Penny, Spike and Milligan did a little dance on the spot.

Troy Cettafax glared at the Zoo Director, then Ralph, Sarah and Bert, before storming off.

The Mayor also turned to leave, but the Zoo Director called him back.

'There's one more thing, Mr Mayor.'

'Yes?' said the Mayor.

'I received another petition this morning, suggesting that we build a new exhibit at the zoo,' continued the Zoo Director, 'for native Irish animals.'

Bob, Fearful Fionnuala, Ralph, Sarah and Bert all looked at each other in surprise. Spike and Milligan looked at Penny, who smiled knowingly.

'It appears all the animals signed it,' said the Zoo Director, holding up the petition Penny and her new friends had organised. 'I found it on the mat outside my office this morning. Now, since I'm the last to leave and the first to arrive every day, I can only assume that the animals actually put this together themselves.'

The Mayor looked at the Zoo Director with disbelief.

'I think it's a great idea!'

said Sarah.

'I agree,' said Fearful Fionnuala who found Irish animals a lot less frightening than lions, orangutans and pandas.

'I think I can find some money in the budget,' said the Mayor.

'Hooray!' cried Spike and Milligan, doing a rendition of Riverdance which was cut short by Bob picking them up.

'And look – here are our first residents,' said Bob, holding Spike and Milligan carefully.

Penny lay stock still on the ground.

'Ralph!' said Sarah. 'Isn't this your pencil? The one the orangutans stole?'

Sarah picked up Penny and handed her to Ralph.

'Yes!' said Ralph, unzipping his pencil case and putting Penny inside.

'Penny!' cried Smudge.

'Am I glad to see you!' said Mack with a huge

sigh of relief.

'What happened? You were gone so long … Are you all right?' asked Gloop.

Penny quickly filled them in on her adventures with Black Texta, Spike and Milligan.

'Do you think Black Texta really will come back?' asked Smudge.

'Herby seemed to think so,' said Penny, 'but maybe as a dung beetle,' she added with a chortle.

'Black Texta's a pretty silly name for a dung beetle if you ask me,' laughed Mack.

'That's great news about the Irish animal exhibit, Penny,' said Gloop. 'With all that was going on you still managed to do something nice for your new friends. I'm very proud.'

'Thanks, Gloop,' said Penny, blushing.

'A big cheer for Penny,' said Mack. 'Hip hip …'

'Hooray!' chorused Smudge, Gloop and all the coloured pencils.

CAVAN COUNTY LIBRARY